GEORGE and SOPHIE'S MUSEUM ADVENTURE

THOMAS TAYLOR

ORCHARD BOOKS

For Oliver and Gabriel

Orchard Books
96 Leonard Street, London EC2A 4XD
Orchard Books Australia
14 Mars Road, Lane Cove, NSW 2066
First published in Great Britain in 1999
This edition published in 2000
ISBN 1 86039 883 9 (hardback)
ISBN 1 84121 581 3 (paperback)
© Thomas Taylor 1999
The right of Thomas Talyor to be identified as the author and the illustrator have been
asserted by him in accordance with the Copyright, Designs and Patents Act, 1988.
A CIP catalogue record for this book is available from the British Library
1 3 5 7 9 10 8 6 4 2 (hardback)
1 3 5 7 9 10 8 6 4 2 (paperback)
Printed in Dubai

Last Thursday, after school, Grandpa took
George and Sophie to the museum.

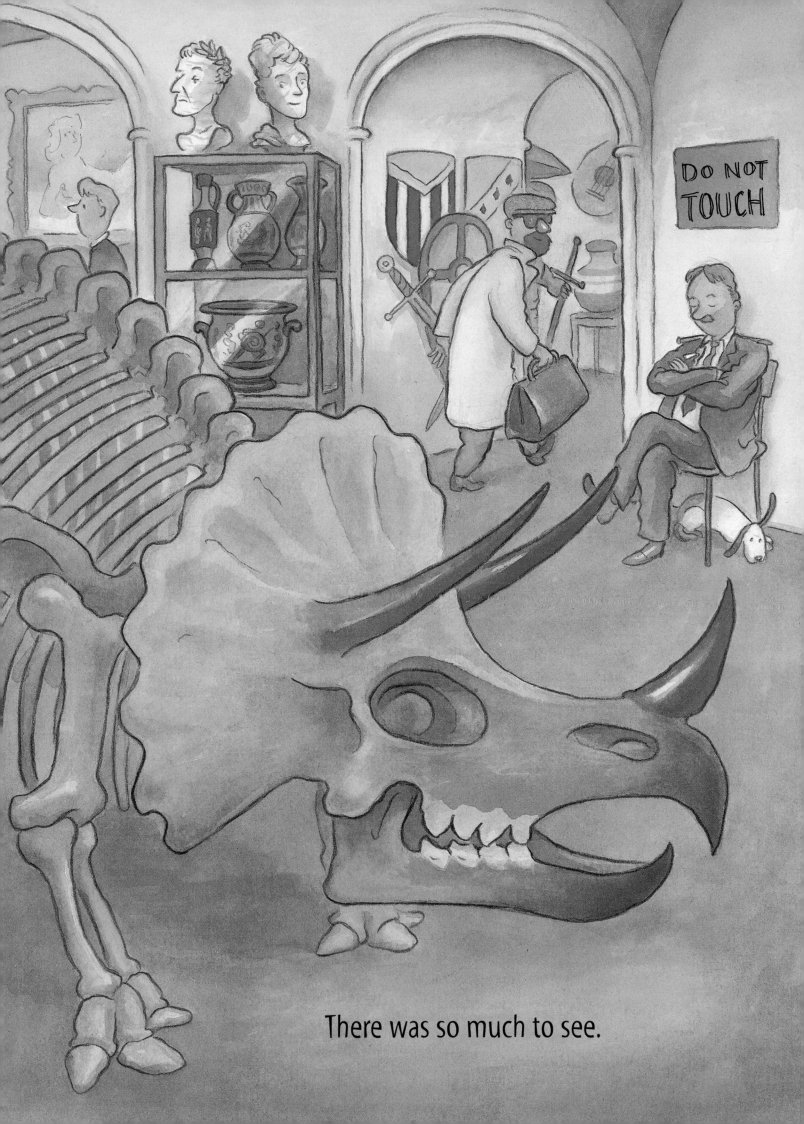

There was so much to see.

George liked the dinosaurs best.

Sophie liked them too, but thought
the African masks were better.

They both liked the paintings.

And Grandpa seemed to know so much
about EVERYTHING.

But the adventure really began when Sophie
saw something very strange.

It was a burglar.
No one else seemed to notice.

George and Sophie ran to tell Grandpa.

But Grandpa didn't believe them.
"Maybe he works here," he said.
"I just know he's a burglar," said Sophie.

George thought they should tell the guard.

Sophie and George wondered what to do next.
The museum was about to close.

But Grandpa just told them to go outside,
while he went to the cloakroom to get their coats.

They watched for the burglar but they didn't see him leave.
It was getting dark.

"If no one believes us," said George, "then we are just going to have to catch the burglar ourselves."

So with some help from a friend, and without waiting for Grandpa, George and Sophie crept back into the museum ...

WOOF!

WOOF!

sssh!

where it was very dark ...

It's different with the lights off.

and very very quiet.

But then they saw their friend again ...

George and Sophie looked very hard,
but they couldn't see the burglar.

But they couldn't find the burglar.

Then George noticed something. A shadow!

George and Sophie followed as quietly as they could.

"What are we going to do?" whispered George.

Hey! What's that?

It's a torch.

Then Sophie had an idea.

What a fright the burglar had!
He was still lying on the floor when Grandpa suddenly appeared.
"I've been looking for you for hours!" cried Grandpa.

The guard arrested the burglar and Sophie
explained what they did.

And that was the end of it all.
The police came and took the burglar away
and Grandpa took George and Sophie home . . .

where they dreamed of their museum adventure.
Did you see these things too?